STORIES

IN WHICH

A House Is Built at Pooh Corner for Eeyore

(*from* THE HOUSE AT POOH CORNER)

IN WHICH

Piglet Is Entirely Surrounded by Water

(*from* WINNIE-THE-POOH)

IN WHICH

Pooh Invents a New Game and Eeyore Joins In

(*from* THE HOUSE AT POOH CORNER)

TORY BOOK

with decorations
and illustrations in full colour
by E. H. SHEPARD

METHUEN

First published in Great Britain 1967
by Methuen & Co Ltd
Reprinted twice
Methuen paperback edition first published 1975
by Methuen Children's Books Ltd
Reprinted 1976, 1977
This edition published simultaneously in hardback and paperback
1982 by Methuen Children's Books Ltd
11 New Fetter Lane, London EC4P 4EE
Paperback edition reprinted 1982 and 1983
Compilation and new illustrations copyright © 1965
E. P. Dutton & Co Inc
Printed in Great Britain by
William Clowes (Beccles) Ltd, Beccles and London
ISBN 0 416 80610 4 (*paperback*)
ISBN 0 416 66370 2 (*hardback*)

IN WHICH A House Is Built at Pooh Corner for Eeyore

ONE DAY when Pooh Bear had nothing else to do, he thought he would do something, so he went round to Piglet's house to see what Piglet was doing. It was still snowing as he stumped over the white forest track, and he expected to find Piglet warming his toes in front of his fire, but to his surprise he saw that the door was open, and the more he looked inside the more Piglet wasn't there.

"He's out," said Pooh sadly. "That's what it is. He's not in. I shall have to go a fast Thinking Walk by myself. Bother!"

But first he thought that he would knock very loudly just to make *quite* sure . . . and while he waited for Piglet not to answer, he jumped up and down to keep warm, and a hum came suddenly into his head, which seemed to him a Good Hum, such as is Hummed Hopefully to Others.

> The more it snows
>   (Tiddely pom),
>   The more it goes
>   (Tiddely pom),
>   The more it goes
>   (Tiddely pom),
>   On snowing.
>   And nobody knows
>   (Tiddely pom),
>   How cold my toes
>   (Tiddely pom),
>   How cold my toes
>   (Tiddely pom),
>   Are growing.

· "So what I'll do," said Pooh, "is I'll do this. I'll just go home first and see what the time is, and perhaps I'll put a muffler round my neck, and then I'll go and see Eeyore and sing it to him."

He hurried back to his own house; and his mind was so busy on the way with the hum that he was getting ready for Eeyore that, when he suddenly saw Piglet sitting in his best arm-chair, he could only stand there rubbing his head and wondering whose house he was in.

"Hallo, Piglet," he said. "I thought you were out."

"No," said Piglet, "it's you who were out, Pooh."

"So it was," said Pooh. "I knew one of us was."

He looked up at his clock, which had stopped at five minutes to eleven some weeks ago.

"Nearly eleven o'clock," said Pooh happily. "You're

just in time for a little smackerel of something," and he put his head into the cupboard. "And then we'll go out, Piglet, and sing my song to Eeyore."

"Which song, Pooh?"

"The one we're going to sing to Eeyore," explained Pooh.

The clock was still saying five minutes to eleven when Pooh and Piglet set out on their way half an hour later. The wind had dropped, and the snow, tired of rushing round in circles trying to catch itself up, now fluttered gently down until it found a place on which to rest, and sometimes the place was Pooh's nose and sometimes it wasn't, and in a little while Piglet was wearing a white muffler round his neck and feeling more snowy behind the ears than he had ever felt before.

"Pooh," he said at last, and a little timidly, because he didn't want Pooh to think he was Giving In, "I was just wondering. How would it be if we went home now and *practised* your song, and then sang it to Eeyore to-morrow – or – or the next day, when we happen to see him?"

"That's a very good idea, Piglet," said Pooh. "We'll practise it now as we go along. But it's no good going home to practise it, because it's a special Outdoor Song which Has To Be Sung In The Snow."

"Are you sure?" asked Piglet anxiously.

"Well, you'll see, Piglet, when you listen. Because

this is how it begins. *The more it snows, tiddely pom* ——"

"Tiddely what?" said Piglet.

"Pom," said Pooh. "I put that in to make it more hummy. *The more it goes, tiddely pom, the more* ——"

"Didn't you say snows?"

"Yes, but that was *before*."

"Before the tiddely pom?"

"It was a *different* tiddely pom," said Pooh, feeling rather muddled now. "I'll sing it to you properly and then you'll see."

So he sang it again.

The more it
SNOWS-tiddely-pom,
The more it
GOES-tiddely-pom
The more it
GOES-tiddely-pom
On
Snowing.

And nobody
KNOWS-tiddely-pom,
How cold my
TOES-tiddely-pom
How cold my
TOES-tiddely-pom
Are
Growing.

He sang it like that, which is much the best way of singing it, and when he had finished, he waited for Piglet to say that, of all the Outdoor Hums for Snowy Weather he had ever heard, this was the best. And, after thinking the matter out carefully, Piglet said:

"Pooh," he said solemnly, "it isn't the *toes* so much as the *ears*."

By this time they were getting near Eeyore's Gloomy Place, which was where he lived, and as it was still very snowy behind Piglet's ears, and he was getting tired of it, they turned into a little pine wood, and sat down on the gate which led into it. They were out of the snow now, but it was very cold, and to keep themselves warm they sang Pooh's song right through six times, Piglet doing the tiddely-poms and Pooh

doing the rest of it, and both of them thumping on
the top of the gate with pieces of stick at the proper
places. And in a little while they felt much warmer,
and were able to talk again.

"I've been thinking," said Pooh, "and what I've
been thinking is this. I've been thinking about
Eeyore."

"What about Eeyore?"

"Well, poor Eeyore has nowhere to live."

"Nor he has," said Piglet.

"*You* have a house, Piglet, and I have a house, and they are very good houses. And Christopher Robin has a house, and Owl and Kanga and Rabbit have houses, and even Rabbit's friends and relations have houses or somethings, but poor Eeyore has nothing. So what I've been thinking is: Let's build him a house."

"That," said Piglet, "is a Grand Idea. Where shall we build it?"

"We will build it here," said Pooh, "just by this wood, out of the wind, because this is where I thought of it. And we will call this Pooh Corner. And we will build an Eeyore House with sticks at Pooh Corner for Eeyore."

"There was a heap of sticks on the other side of the wood," said Piglet. "I saw them. Lots and lots. All piled up."

"Thank you, Piglet," said Pooh. "What you have just said will be a Great Help to us, and because of it I could call this place Poohanpiglet Corner if Pooh

Corner didn't sound better, which it does, being smaller and more like a corner. Come along."

So they got down off the gate and went round to the other side of the wood to fetch the sticks.

Christopher Robin had spent the morning indoors going to Africa and back, and he had just got off the boat and was wondering what it was like outside, when who should come knocking at the door but Eeyore.

"Hallo, Eeyore," said Christopher Robin, as he opened the door and came out. "How are *you?*"

"It's snowing still," said Eeyore gloomily.

"So it is."

"*And* freezing."

"Is it?"

"Yes," said Eeyore. "How-
ever," he said, brightening up
a little, "we haven't had an earthquake lately."

"What's the matter, Eeyore?"

"Nothing, Christopher Robin. Nothing important.
I suppose you haven't seen a house or what-not any-
where about?"

"What sort of a house?"

"Just a house."

"Who lives there?"

"I do. At least I thought I did. But I suppose I don't.
After all, we can't all have houses."

"But, Eeyore, I didn't know – I always thought
____"

"I don't know how it is, Christopher Robin, but
what with all this snow and one thing and another,
not to mention icicles and such-like, it isn't so Hot in
my field about three o'clock in the morning as some

people think it is. It isn't Close, if you know what I mean – not so as to be uncomfortable. It isn't Stuffy. In fact, Christopher Robin," he went on in a loud whisper, "quite-between-ourselves-and-don't-tell-anybody, it's Cold."

"Oh, Eeyore!"

"And I said to myself: The others will be sorry if I'm getting myself all cold. They haven't got Brains, any of them, only grey fluff that's blown into their heads by mistake, and they don't Think, but if it goes on snowing for another six weeks or so, one of them will begin to say to himself: 'Eeyore can't be so very much too Hot about three o'clock in the morning.' And then it will Get About. And they'll be Sorry."

"Oh, Eeyore!" said Christopher Robin, feeling very sorry already.

"I don't mean you, Christopher Robin. You're different. So what it all comes to is that I built myself a house down by my little wood."

"Did you really? How exciting!"

"The really exciting part," said Eeyore in his most melancholy voice, "is that when I left it this morning it was there, and when I came back it wasn't. Not at all, very natural, and it was only Eeyore's house. But still I just wondered."

Christopher Robin didn't stop to wonder. He was already back in *his* house, putting on his waterproof hat, his waterproof boots and his waterproof macintosh as fast as he could.

"We'll go and look for it at once," he called out to Eeyore.

"Sometimes," said Eeyore, "when people have quite finished taking a person's house, there are one or two bits which they don't want and are rather glad for the person to take back, if you know what I mean. So I thought if we just went —"

"Come on," said Christopher Robin, and off they hurried, and in a very little time they got to the corner of the field by the side of the pine wood, where Eeyore's house wasn't any longer.

"There!" said Eeyore. "Not a stick of it left! Of course, I've still got all this snow to do what I like with. One mustn't complain."

But Christopher Robin wasn't listening to Eeyore, he was listening to something else.

"Can you hear it?" he asked.

"What is it? Somebody laughing?"

"Listen."

They both listened . . . and they heard a deep gruff voice saying in a singing voice that the more it snowed the more it went on snowing and a small high voice tiddely-pomming in between.

"It's Pooh," said Christopher Robin excitedly. . . .

"Possibly," said Eeyore.

"*And* Piglet!" said Christopher Robin excitedly.

"Probably," said Eeyore. "What we *want* is a Trained Bloodhound."

The words of the song changed suddenly.

"*We've finished our HOUSE!*" sang the gruff voice.

"*Tiddely pom!*" sang the squeaky one.

"It's a beautiful HOUSE . . ."
"Tiddely pom . . ."
"I wish it were MINE. . . ."
"Tiddely pom. . . ."
"Pooh!" shouted Christopher Robin. . . .
The singers on the gate stopped suddenly.
"It's Christopher Robin!" said Pooh eagerly.
"He's round by the place where we got all those sticks from," said Piglet.
"Come on," said Pooh.

They climbed down their gate and hurried round the corner of the wood, Pooh making welcoming noises all the way.

"Why, here *is* Eeyore," said Pooh, when he had finished hugging Christopher Robin, and he nudged Piglet, and Piglet nudged him, and they thought to themselves what a lovely surprise they had got ready. "Hallo, Eeyore."

"Same to you, Pooh Bear, and twice on Thursdays," said Eeyore gloomily.

Before Pooh could say: "Why Thursdays?" Christopher Robin began to explain the sad story of Eeyore's Lost House. And Pooh and Piglet listened, and their eyes seemed to get bigger and bigger.

"*Where* did you say it was?" asked Pooh.

"Just here," said Eeyore.

"Made of sticks?"

"Yes."

"Oh!" said Piglet.

"What?" said Eeyore.

"I just said 'Oh!' " said Piglet nervously. And so as to seem quite at ease he hummed tiddely-pom once or twice in a what-shall-we-do-now kind of way.

"You're sure it *was* a house?" said Pooh. "I mean, you're sure the house was just here?"

"Of course I am," said Eeyore. And he murmured to himself, "No brain at all, some of them."

"Why, what's the matter, Pooh?" asked Christopher Robin.

"Well," said Pooh. . . . "The fact *is*," said Pooh . . . "Well, the fact *is*," said Pooh . . . "You see," said Pooh. . . . "It's like this," said Pooh, and something seemed to tell him that he wasn't explaining very well, and he nudged Piglet again.

"It's like this," said Piglet quickly. . . . "Only warmer," he added after deep thought.

"What's warmer?"

"The other side of the wood, where Eeyore's house is."

"*My* house?" said Eeyore. "My house was here."

"No," said Piglet firmly. "The other side of the wood."

"Because of being warmer," said Pooh.

"But I ought to *know* ——"

"Come and look," said Piglet simply, and he led
the way.

"There wouldn't be *two* houses," said Pooh. "Not
so close together."

They came round the corner, and there was Eeyore's house, looking as comfy as anything.

"There you are," said Piglet.
"Inside as well as outside," said Pooh proudly.

Eeyore went inside . . . and came out again.

"It's a remarkable thing," he said. "It *is* my house, and I built it where I said I did, so the wind must have blown it here. And the wind blew it right over the wood, and blew it down here, and here it is as good as ever. In fact, better in places."

"Much better," said Pooh and Piglet together.

"It just shows what can be done by taking a little trouble," said Eeyore. "Do you see, Pooh? Do you see, Piglet? Brains first and then Hard Work. Look at it! *That's* the way to build a house," said Eeyore proudly.

So they left him in it; and Christopher Robin went back to lunch with his friends Pooh and Piglet, and on the way they told him of the Awful Mistake they had made. And when he had finished laughing, they all sang the Outdoor Song for Snowy Weather the rest of the way home, Piglet, who was still not quite sure of his voice, putting in the tiddely-poms again.

"And I know it *seems* easy," said Piglet to himself, "but it isn't *every one* who could do it."

IN WHICH Piglet Is Entirely Surrounded by Water

IT RAINED and it rained and it rained. Piglet told himself that never in all his life, and *he* was goodness knows *how* old – three, was it, or four? – never had he seen so much rain. Days and days and days.

"If only," he thought, as he looked out of the window, "I had been in Pooh's house, or Christopher Robin's house, or Rabbit's house when it began to rain, then I should have had Company all this time, instead of being here all alone, with nothing to do except wonder when it will stop." And he imagined himself with Pooh, saying, "Did you ever see such rain, Pooh?" and Pooh saying, "Isn't it *awful*, Piglet?" and Piglet saying, "I wonder how it is over Christopher Robin's way," and Pooh saying, "I should think poor old Rabbit is about flooded out by this time." It would have been jolly to talk like this, and really, it wasn't much good having anything exciting like floods, if you couldn't share them with somebody.

For it was rather exciting. The little dry ditches in which Piglet had nosed about so often had become streams, the little streams across which he had splashed were rivers, and the river, between whose steep banks they had played so happily, had sprawled out of its own bed and was taking up so much room every-where, that Piglet was beginning to wonder whether it would be coming into *his* bed soon.

"It's a little Anxious," he said to himself, "to be a Very Small Animal Entirely Surrounded by Water. Christopher Robin and Pooh could escape by Climb-ing Trees, and Kanga could escape by Jumping, and Rabbit could escape by Burrowing, and Owl could escape by Flying, and Eeyore could escape by – by Making a Loud Noise Until Rescued, and here am I, surrounded by water and I can't do *anything*."

It went on raining, and every day the water got a

little higher, until now it was nearly up to Piglet's
window . . . and still he hadn't done anything.

"There's Pooh," he thought to himself. "Pooh
hasn't much Brain, but he never comes to any harm.
He does silly things and they turn out right. There's
Owl. Owl hasn't exactly got Brain, but he Knows
Things. He would know the Right Thing to Do
when Surrounded by Water. There's Rabbit. He
hasn't Learnt in Books, but he can always Think of
a Clever Plan. There's Kanga. She isn't Clever,
Kanga isn't, but she would be so anxious about Roo
that she would do a Good Thing to Do without

thinking about it. And then there's Eeyore. And Eeyore is so miserable anyhow that he wouldn't mind about this. But I wonder what Christopher Robin would do?"

Then suddenly he remembered a story which Christopher Robin had told him about a man on a desert island who had written something in a bottle and thrown it into the sea; and Piglet thought that if he wrote something in a bottle and threw it in the water, perhaps somebody would come and rescue *him!*

He left the window and began to search his house, all of it that wasn't under water, and at last he found a pencil and a small piece of dry paper, and a bottle with a cork to it. And he wrote on one side of the paper:

HELP!

PIGLIT (ME)

and on the other side:

IT'S ME PIGLIT, HELP HELP!

Then he put the paper in the bottle, and he corked the bottle up as tightly as he could, and he leant out of his window as far as he could lean without falling in, and he threw the bottle as far as he could throw – *splash!* – and in a little while it bobbed up again on the water; and he watched it floating slowly away in the distance, until his eyes ached with looking, and sometimes he thought it was the bottle, and sometimes he thought it was just a ripple on the water which he was following, and then suddenly he knew that he would never see it again and that he had done all that he could do to save himself.

"So now," he thought, "somebody else will have to do something, and I hope they will do it soon, because if they don't I shall have to swim, which I can't, so I hope they do it soon." And then he gave a very long sigh and said, "I wish Pooh were here. It's so much more friendly with two."

When the rain began Pooh was asleep. It rained, and it rained, and it rained, and he slept and he slept and he slept. He had had a tiring day. You remember how he discovered the North Pole; well, he was so proud of this that he asked Christopher Robin if there were any other Poles such as a Bear of Little Brain might discover.

"There's a South Pole," said Christopher Robin, "and I expect there's an East Pole and a West Pole, though people don't like talking about them."

Pooh was very excited when he heard this, and suggested that they should have an Expotition to discover the East Pole, but Christopher Robin had thought of something else to do with Kanga; so Pooh went out to discover the East Pole by himself. Whether he discovered it or not, I forget; but he was so tired when he got home that, in the very middle of his supper, after he had been eating for little more than half-an-hour, he fell fast asleep in his chair, and slept and slept and slept.

Then suddenly he was dreaming. He was at the East Pole, and it was a very cold pole with the coldest sort of snow and ice all over it. He had found a bee-hive to sleep in, but there wasn't room for his legs,

so he had left them outside. And **Wild Woozles**, such
as inhabit the East Pole, came and nibbled all the fur
off his legs to make Nests for their Young. And the
more they nibbled, the colder his legs got, until
suddenly he woke up with an *Ow!* – and there he

was, sitting in his chair with his feet in the water, and water all round him!

He splashed to his door and looked out. . . .

"This is Serious," said Pooh. "I must have an Escape."

So he took his largest pot of honey and escaped
with it to a broad branch of his tree, well above the
water, and then he climbed down again and escaped
with another pot . . . and when the whole Escape
was finished, there was Pooh sitting on his branch,
dangling his legs, and there, beside him, were ten pots
of honey. . . .

Two days later, there was Pooh, sitting on his
branch, dangling his legs, and there, beside him, were
four pots of honey. . . .

Three days later, there was Pooh, sitting on his

branch, dangling his legs, and there, beside him, was one pot of honey.

Four days later, there was Pooh . . .

And it was on the morning of the fourth day that Piglet's bottle came floating past him, and with one loud cry of "Honey!" Pooh plunged into the water, seized the bottle, and struggled back to his tree again.

"Bother!" said Pooh, as he opened it. "All that wet for nothing. What's that bit of paper doing?"

He took it out and looked at it.

"It's a Missage," he said to himself, "that's what it is. And that letter is a 'P,' and so is that, and so is that, and 'P' means 'Pooh,' so it's a very important Missage to me, and I can't read it. I must find Christopher Robin or Owl or Piglet, one of those Clever Readers who can read things, and they will tell me what this message means. Only I can't swim. Bother!"

Then he had an idea, and I think that for a Bear of Very Little Brain, it was a good idea. He said to himself:

"If a bottle can float, then a jar can float, and if a jar floats, I can sit on the top of it, if it's a very big jar."

So he took his biggest jar, and corked it up. "All boats have to have a name," he said, "so I shall call

mine *The Floating Bear*." And with these words he dropped his boat into the water and jumped in after it.

For a little while Pooh and *The Floating Bear* were uncertain as to which of them was meant to be on the top, but after trying one or two different positions,

they settled down with *The Floating Bear* underneath
and Pooh triumphantly astride it, paddling vigorously
with his feet.

Christopher Robin lived at the very top of the Forest. It rained, and it rained, and it rained, but the water couldn't come up to *his* house. It was rather jolly to look down into the valleys and see the water all round him, but it rained so hard that he stayed indoors most of the time, and thought about things. Every morning he went out with his umbrella and put a stick in the place where the water came up to, and every next morning he went out and couldn't see his stick any more, so he put another stick in the place where the water came up to, and then he walked home again, and each morning he had a shorter way to walk than he had had the morning before. On the morning of the fifth day he saw the water all round him, and knew that for the first time in his life he was on a real island. Which was very exciting.

It was on this morning that Owl came flying over the water to say "How do you do," to his friend Christopher Robin.

"I say, Owl," said Christopher Robin, "isn't this fun? I'm on an island!"

"The atmospheric conditions have been very un-favourable lately," said Owl.

"The what?"

"It has been raining," explained Owl.

"Yes," said Christopher Robin. "It has."

"The flood-level has reached an unprecedented height."

"The who?"

"There's a lot of water about," explained Owl.

"Yes," said Christopher Robin, "there is."

"However, the prospects are rapidly becoming more favourable. At any moment – "

"Have you seen Pooh?"

"No. At any moment – "

"I hope he's all right," said Christopher Robin. "I've been wondering about him. I expect Piglet's with him. Do you think they're all right, Owl?"

"I expect so. You see, at any moment – "

"Do go and see, Owl. Because Pooh hasn't got very much brain, and he might do something silly, and I do love him so, Owl. Do you see, Owl?"

"That's all right," said Owl. "I'll go. Back directly." And he flew off.

In a little while he was back again.

"Pooh isn't there," he said.

"Not there?"

"Has *been* there. He's been sitting on a branch of his tree outside his house with nine pots of honey. But he isn't there now."

"Oh, Pooh!" cried Christopher Robin. "Where *are* you?"

"Here I am," said a growly voice behind him.

"Pooh!"

They rushed into each other's arms.

"How did you get here, Pooh?" asked Christopher Robin, when he was ready to talk again.

"On my boat," said Pooh proudly. "I had a Very Important Missage sent me in a bottle, and owing to having got some water in my eyes, I couldn't read it, so I brought it to you. On my boat."

With these proud words he gave Christopher Robin the missage.

"But it's from Piglet!" cried Christopher Robin when he had read it.

"Isn't there anything about Pooh in it?" asked Bear, looking over his shoulder.

Christopher Robin read the message aloud.

"Oh, are those 'P's' Piglets? I thought they were Poohs."

"We must rescue him at once! I thought he was with *you,* Pooh. Owl, could you rescue him on your back?"

"I don't think so," said Owl, after grave thought. "It is doubtful if the necessary dorsal muscles ——"

"Then would you fly to him at *once* and say that Rescue is Coming? And Pooh and I will think of a Rescue and come as quick as ever we can. Oh, don't *talk,* Owl, go on quick!" And, still thinking of something to say, Owl flew off.

"Now then, Pooh," said Christopher Robin, "where's your boat?"

"I ought to say," explained Pooh as they walked down to the shore of the island, "that it isn't just an ordinary sort of boat. Sometimes it's a Boat, and sometimes it's more of an Accident. It all depends."

"Depends on what?"

"On whether I'm on the top of it or underneath it."

"Oh! Well, where is it?"

"There!" said Pooh, pointing proudly to *The Floating Bear.*

It wasn't what Christopher Robin expected, and the more he looked at it, the more he thought what a Brave and Clever Bear Pooh was, and the more Christopher Robin thought this, the more Pooh looked modestly down his nose and tried to pretend he wasn't.

"But it's too small for two of us," said Christopher Robin sadly.

"Three of us with Piglet."

"That makes it smaller still. Oh, Pooh Bear, what shall we do?"

And then this Bear, Pooh Bear, Winnie-the-Pooh, F.O.P. (Friend of Piglet's), R.C. (Rabbit's Companion), P.D. (Pole Discoverer), E.C. and T.F. (Eeyore's Comforter and Tail-finder) – in fact, Pooh himself – said something so clever that Christopher Robin could only look at him with mouth open and eyes staring, wondering if this was really the Bear of Very Little Brain whom he had known and loved so long.

"We might go in your umbrella," said Pooh.

"?"

"We might go in your umbrella," said Pooh.

"? ?"

"We might go in your umbrella," said Pooh.

"! ! ! ! ! !"

For suddenly Christopher Robin saw that they might. He opened his umbrella and put it point

downwards in the water. It floated but wobbled.
Pooh got in. He was just beginning to say that it was
all right now, when he found that it wasn't, so after a
short drink, which he didn't really want, he waded
back to Christopher Robin. Then they both got in
together, and it wobbled no longer.

"I shall call this boat *The Brain of Pooh*," said
Christopher Robin, and *The Brain of Pooh* set sail
forthwith in a south-westerly direction, revolving
gracefully.

You can imagine Piglet's joy when at last the ship
came in sight of him. In after-years he liked to think
that he had been in Very Great Danger during the
Terrible Flood, but the only danger he had really
been in was in the last half-hour of his imprisonment,
when Owl, who had just flown up, sat on a branch
of his tree to comfort him, and told him a very long
story about an aunt who had once laid a seagull's egg

by mistake, and the story went on and on, rather like this sentence, until Piglet, who was listening out of his window without much hope, went to sleep quietly and naturally, slipping slowly out of the window towards the water until he was only hanging on by his toes, at which moment, luckily, a sudden loud squawk from Owl, which was really part of the story, being what his aunt said, woke the Piglet up and just gave him time to jerk himself back into safety and say, "How interesting, and did she?" when – well, you can imagine his joy when at last he saw the good ship *Brain of Pooh* (*Captain,* C. Robin; *1st Mate,* P. Bear) coming over the sea to rescue him. . . .

And as that is really the end of the story, and I am very tired after that last sentence, I think I shall stop there.

IN WHICH Pooh Invents a New Game and Eeyore Joins In

B Y THE time it came to the edge of the Forest the stream had grown up, so that it was almost a river, and, being grown-up, it did not run and jump and sparkle along as it used to do when it was younger, but moved more slowly. For it knew now where it was going, and it said to itself, "There is no hurry. We shall get there some day." But all the little streams higher up in the Forest went this way and that, quickly, eagerly, having so much to find out before it was too late.

There was a broad track, almost as broad as a road, leading from the Outland to the Forest, but before it could come to the Forest, it had to cross this river. So, where it crossed, there was a wooden bridge, almost as broad as a road, with wooden rails each side of it. Christopher Robin could just get his chin on to the top rail, if he wanted to, but it was more fun to stand on the bottom rail, so that he could lean right over, and watch the river slipping slowly away beneath him. Pooh could get his chin on to the bottom rail if he wanted to, but it was more fun to lie down and get his head under it, and watch the river slipping slowly away beneath him. And this was the only way in which Piglet and Roo could watch the river at all, because they were too small to reach the bottom rail. So they would lie down and watch it . . . and it slipped away very slowly, being in no hurry to get there.

One day, when Pooh was walking towards this bridge, he was trying to make up a piece of poetry about fir-cones, because there they were, lying about on each side of him, and he felt singy. So he picked a fir-cone up, and looked at it, and said to himself, "This is a very good fir-cone, and something ought to rhyme to it." But he couldn't think of anything. And then this came into his head suddenly:

Here is a myst'ry
About a little fir-tree.
Owl says it's *his* tree,
And Kanga says it's *her* tree.

"Which doesn't make sense," said Pooh, "because Kanga doesn't live in a tree."

He had just come to the bridge; and not looking where he was going, he tripped over something, and the fir-cone jerked out of his paw into the river.

"Bother," said Pooh, as it floated slowly under the bridge, and he went back to get another fir-cone which had a rhyme to it. But then he thought that he would just look at the river instead, because it was a peaceful sort of day, so he lay down and looked at it, and it slipped slowly away beneath him . . . and suddenly, there was his fir-cone slipping away too.

"That's funny," said Pooh. "I dropped it on the other side," said Pooh, "and it came out on this side! I wonder if it would do it again?" And he went back for some more fir-cones.

It did. It kept on doing it. Then he dropped two
in at once, and leant over the bridge to see which of
them would come out first; and one of them did; but
as they were both the same size, he didn't know if it
was the one which he wanted to win, or the other
one. So the next time he dropped one big one and
one little one, and the big one came out first, which
was what he had said it would do, and the little one

came out last, which was what he had said it would do, so he had won twice . . . and when he went home for tea, he had won thirty-six and lost twenty-eight, which meant that he was – that he had – well, you take twenty-eight from thirty-six, and *that's* what he was. Instead of the other way round.

And that was the beginning of the game called Poohsticks, which Pooh invented, and which he and his friends used to play on the edge of the Forest. But they played with sticks instead of fir-cones, because they were easier to mark.

Now one day Pooh and Piglet and Rabbit and Roo were all playing Poohsticks together. They had dropped their sticks in when Rabbit said "Go!" and then they had hurried across to the other side of the bridge, and now they were all leaning over the edge, waiting to see whose stick would come out first. But it was a long time coming, because the river was very lazy that day, and hardly seemed to mind if it didn't ever get there at all.

"I can see mine!" cried Roo. "No, I can't, it's something else. Can you see yours, Piglet? I thought I could see mine, but I couldn't. There it is! No, it isn't. Can you see yours, Pooh?"

"No," said Pooh.

"I expect my stick's stuck," said Roo. "Rabbit, my stick's stuck. Is your stick stuck, Piglet?"

"They always take longer than you think," said Rabbit.

"How long do you *think* they'll take?" asked Roo.

"I can see yours, Piglet," said Pooh suddenly.

"Mine's a sort of greyish one," said Piglet, not daring to lean too far over in case he fell in.

"Yes, that's what I can see. It's coming over on to my side."

Rabbit leant over further than ever, looking for

his, and Roo wriggled up and down, calling out "Come on, stick! Stick, stick, stick!" and Piglet got very excited because his was the only one which had been seen, and that meant that he was winning.

"It's coming!" said Pooh.

"Are you *sure* it's mine?" squeaked Piglet excitedly.

"Yes, because it's grey. A big grey one. Here it comes! A very - big - grey —— Oh, no, it isn't, it's Eeyore."

And out floated Eeyore.

"Eeyore!" cried everybody.

Looking very calm, very dignified, with his legs in the air, came Eeyore from beneath the bridge.

"It's Eeyore!" cried Roo, terribly excited.

"Is that so?" said Eeyore, getting caught up by a little eddy, and turning slowly round three times. "I wondered."

"I didn't know you were playing," said Roo.

"I'm not," said Eeyore.

"Eeyore, what *are* you doing there?" said Rabbit.

"I'll give you three guesses, Rabbit. Digging holes in the ground? Wrong. Leaping from branch to branch of a young oak-tree? Wrong. Waiting for somebody to help me out of the river? Right. Give Rabbit time, and he'll always get the answer."

"But, Eeyore," said Pooh in distress, "what can we - I mean, how shall we - do you think if we ——"

"Yes," said Eeyore. "One of those would be just the thing. Thank you, Pooh."

"He's going *round* and *round*," said Roo, much impressed.

"And why not?" said Eeyore coldly.

"I can swim too," said Roo proudly.

"Not round and round," said Eeyore. "It's much more difficult. I didn't want to come swimming at all to-day," he went on, revolving slowly. "But if, when in, I decide to practise a slight circular movement from right to left – or perhaps I should say," he added, as he got into another eddy, "from left to right, just as it happens to occur to me, it is nobody's business but my own."

There was a moment's silence while everybody thought.

"I've got a sort of idea," said Pooh at last, "but I don't suppose it's a very good one."

"I don't suppose it is either," said Eeyore.

"Go on, Pooh," said Rabbit. "Let's have it."

"Well, if we all threw stones and things into the river on *one* side of Eeyore, the stones would make waves, and the waves would wash him to the other side."

"That's a very good idea," said Rabbit, and Pooh looked happy again.

"Very," said Eeyore. "When I want to be washed, Pooh, I'll let you know."

"Supposing we hit him by mistake?" said Piglet anxiously.

"Or supposing you missed him by mistake," said Eeyore. "Think of all the possibilities, Piglet, before you settle down to enjoy yourselves."

But Pooh had got the biggest stone he could carry, and was leaning over the bridge, holding it in his paws.

"I'm not throwing it, I'm dropping it, Eeyore," he explained. "And then I can't miss – I mean I can't hit you. *Could* you stop turning round for a moment, because it muddles me rather?"

"No," said Eeyore. "I *like* turning round."

Rabbit began to feel that it was time he took command.

"Now, Pooh," he said, "when I say 'Now!' you can drop it. Eeyore, when I say 'Now!' Pooh will drop his stone."

"Thank you very much, Rabbit, but I expect I shall know."

"Are you ready, Pooh? Piglet, give Pooh a little more room. Get back a bit there, Roo. Are you ready?"

"No," said Eeyore.

"*Now!*" said Rabbit.

Pooh dropped his stone. There was a loud splash, and Eeyore disappeared. . . .

It was an anxious moment for the watchers on the bridge. They looked and looked . . . and even the sight of Piglet's stick coming out a little in front of Rabbit's didn't cheer them up as much as you would have expected. And then, just as Pooh was beginning to think that he must have chosen the wrong stone or the wrong river or the wrong day for his Idea, something grey showed for a moment by the river bank . . . and it got slowly bigger and bigger . . . and at last it was Eeyore coming out.

With a shout they rushed off the bridge, and pushed and pulled at him; and soon he was standing among them again on dry land.

"Oh, Eeyore, you *are* wet!" said Piglet, feeling him.

Eeyore shook himself, and asked somebody to explain to Piglet what happened when you had been inside a river for quite a long time.

"Well done, Pooh," said Rabbit kindly. "That was a good idea of ours."

"What was?" asked Eeyore.

"Hooshing you to the bank like that."

"*Hooshing* me?" said Eeyore in surprise. "Hooshing *me?* You didn't think I was *hooshed,* did you? I dived. Pooh dropped a large stone on me, and so as not to be struck heavily on the chest, I dived and swam to the bank."

"You didn't really," whispered Piglet to Pooh, so as to comfort him.

"I didn't *think* I did," said Pooh anxiously.

"It's just Eeyore," said Piglet. "*I* thought your Idea was a very good Idea."

Pooh began to feel a little more comfortable, because when you are a Bear of Very Little Brain, and you Think of Things, you find sometimes that a Thing which seemed very Thingish inside you is quite different when it gets out into the open and has other people looking at it. And, anyhow, Eeyore *was* in the river, and now he *wasn't,* so he hadn't done any harm.

"How did you fall in, Eeyore?" asked Rabbit, as he dried him with Piglet's handkerchief.

"I didn't," said Eeyore.

"But how ——"

"I was BOUNCED," said Eeyore.

"Oo," said Roo excitedly, "did somebody push you?"

"Somebody BOUNCED me. I was just thinking by the side of the river – thinking, if any of you know what that means – when I received a loud BOUNCE."

"Oh, Eeyore!" said everybody.

"Are you sure you didn't slip?" asked Rabbit wisely.

"Of course I slipped. If you're standing on the

slippery bank of a river, and somebody BOUNCES you loudly from behind, you slip. What did you think I did?"

"But who did it?" asked Roo.

Eeyore didn't answer.

"I expect it was Tigger," said Piglet nervously.

"But, Eeyore," said Pooh, "was it a Joke, or an Accident? I mean ——"

"I didn't stop to ask, Pooh. Even at the very bottom of the river I didn't stop to say to myself, '*Is* this a Hearty Joke, or is it the Merest Accident?' I just floated to the surface, and said to myself, 'It's wet.' If you know what I mean."

"And where was Tigger?" asked Rabbit.

Before Eeyore could answer, there was a loud noise behind them, and through the hedge came Tigger himself.

"Hallo, everybody," said Tigger cheerfully.

"Hallo, Tigger," said Roo.

Rabbit became very important suddenly.

"Tigger," he said solemnly, "what happened just now?"

"Just when?" said Tigger a little uncomfortably.

"When you bounced Eeyore into the river."

"I didn't bounce him."

"You bounced me," said Eeyore gruffly.

"I didn't really. I had a cough, and I happened to be behind Eeyore, and I said '*Grrrr - oppp - ptschschschz.*'"

"Why?" said Rabbit, helping Piglet up, and dusting him. "It's all right, Piglet."

"It took me by surprise," said Piglet nervously.

"That's what I call bouncing," said Eeyore. "Taking people by surprise. Very unpleasant habit. I don't mind Tigger being in the Forest," he went on, "because it's a large Forest, and there's plenty of room to bounce in it. But I don't see why he should come into *my* little corner of it, and bounce there. It isn't as if there was anything very wonderful about my little corner. Of course for people who like cold, wet, ugly bits it *is* something rather special, but otherwise it's just a corner, and if anybody feels bouncy ——"

"I didn't bounce, I coughed," said Tigger crossly.

"Bouncy or coffy, it's all the same at the bottom of the river."

"Well," said Rabbit, "all I can say is – well, here's Christopher Robin, so *he* can say it."

Christopher Robin came down from the Forest to the bridge, feeling all sunny and careless, and just as if twice nineteen didn't matter a bit, as it didn't on such a happy afternoon, and he thought that if he stood on the bottom rail of the bridge, and leant over, and watched the river slipping slowly away

beneath him, then he would suddenly know every-
thing that there was to be known, and he would be
able to tell Pooh, who wasn't quite sure about some
of it. But when he got to the bridge and saw all the

animals there, then he knew that it wasn't that kind of afternoon, but the other kind, when you wanted to *do* something.

"It's like this, Christopher Robin," began Rabbit. "Tigger —"

"No, I didn't," said Tigger.

"Well, anyhow, there I was," said Eeyore.

"But I don't think he meant to," said Pooh.

"He just *is* bouncy," said Piglet, "and he can't help it."

"Try bouncing *me*, Tigger," said Roo eagerly. "Eeyore, Tigger's going to try *me*. Piglet, do you think —"

"Yes, yes," said Rabbit, "we don't all want to speak at once. The point is, what does Christopher Robin think about it?"

"All I did was I coughed," said Tigger.

"He bounced," said Eeyore.

"Well, I sort of boffed," said Tigger.

"Hush!" said Rabbit, holding up his paw. "What does Christopher Robin think about it all? That's the point."

"Well," said Christopher Robin, not quite sure what it was all about, "*I* think —"

"Yes?" said everybody.

"*I* think we all ought to play Poohsticks."

So they did. And Eeyore, who had never played it before, won more times than anybody else; and Roo fell in twice, the first time by accident and the second time on purpose, because he suddenly saw Kanga

coming from the Forest, and he knew he'd have to
go to bed anyhow. So then Rabbit said he'd go with
them; and Tigger and Eeyore went off together,
because Eeyore wanted to tell Tigger How to Win
at Poohsticks, which you do by letting your stick
drop in a twitchy sort of way, if you understand
what I mean, Tigger; and Christopher Robin and
Pooh and Piglet were left on the bridge by themselves.

For a long time they looked at the river beneath them, saying nothing, and the river said nothing too, for it felt very quiet and peaceful on this summer afternoon.

"Tigger is all right, *really*," said Piglet lazily.

"Of course he is," said Christopher Robin.

"Everybody is *really*," said Pooh. "That's what *I* think," said Pooh. "But I don't suppose I'm right," he said.

"Of course you are," said Christopher Robin.

Other books by A. A. Milne
with illustrations by E. H. Shepard

Winnie-the-Pooh
also available with full-colour illustrations throughout
The House at Pooh Corner
also available with full-colour illustrations throughout
When We Were Very Young
Now We Are Six
(these four titles are also in paperback in Magnet Books)
The Hums of Pooh

COLLECTED EDITIONS
The World of Christopher Robin
the complete *When We Were Very Young* and *Now We Are Six*
The World of Pooh
the complete *Winnie-the-Pooh* and *The House at Pooh Corner*
The Christopher Robin Story Book
stories from *Winnie-the-Pooh* and *The House at Pooh Corner*
with verses from *When We Were Very Young* and *Now We Are Six*

FOR YOUNGER READERS
The Christopher Robin Verse Book
twenty-four verses selected from *When We Were Very Young* and
Now We Are Six (also in paperback)
Pooh's Pot o'Honey
four little books, each with a complete story, and all together in a box
Piglet Books
each book is a complete story from *Winnie-the-Pooh* or
The House at Pooh Corner. The text is printed in large,
clear type and all illustrations are in colour (in paperback
in Magnet Books).

Katie Stewart
The Pooh Cook Book
(also in paperback in Magnet Books)
The Pooh Corner Cook Book
Two cook books specially for children

Patsy Kumm
The Pooh Party Book
Suggestions for all kinds of parties, including refreshments

Antony Miall
The Pooh Song Book
Fifteen songs with piano accompaniment and simple guitar chords